The Great Game
The Race

The Great Game - The Race

The Great Game, Volume 1

Syed Makki Shah

Published by El Cid, 2024.

THE GREAT GAME - THE RACE

First edition. September 18, 2024.

Copyright © 2024 Syed Makki Shah.

ISBN: 979-8227039194

Written by Syed Makki Shah.

To Every Warrior of Every Nation

Prologue: The Shockwave

Thar Desert, India – May 1974

The sun crept over the vast dunes of the Thar Desert, casting long, wavering shadows that danced across the barren landscape. A lone shepherd, guiding his flock of goats along a dry riverbed, paused and looked to the horizon. The ground trembled beneath him, a faint vibration at first, like the low rumble of distant thunder. He turned his head, squinting into the sun as if searching for the source of the disturbance.

Then, in an instant, the sky was ripped apart by a blinding flash of light. The shepherd stumbled back, shielding his eyes as a hot wind blew past, carrying with it a wave of dust and sand. He felt the earth shake beneath his feet, and the sound that followed was deafening—a deep, bone-rattling roar that seemed to come from the very core of the earth.

Miles away, in the city of Jaisalmer, windows shattered, and people ran into the streets, fear and confusion etched on their faces. A journalist, recently arrived from Delhi, felt the ground tremble beneath her feet and instinctively reached for her camera, capturing the unfolding chaos. She had heard whispers of a test, rumors of something big happening in the desert, but nothing could have prepared her for this—a nuclear detonation, the first in India's history.

By midday, the news had spread like wildfire across the globe. India had tested a nuclear device, codenamed Operation Smiling Buddha. The world reacted with a mixture of shock, fear, and condemnation. Politicians in London, Moscow, Washington, and Beijing huddled in crisis meetings, weighing their options, calculating their responses. But in Islamabad, the reaction was different. Here, the news was met not with fear but with cold determination and a sense of urgency that cut through the usual bureaucratic inertia like a knife.

Islamabad, Pakistan – The Same Day

Prime Minister Zulfiqar Khan stood by the window of his office, gazing out over the city. His hands were clasped behind his back, his face set in a deep, contemplative frown. The room was filled with the muted hum of an air conditioner, the faint scent of cigarette smoke lingering in the air. Across from him sat General Rahim Javed, his Chief of Army Staff, his posture rigid, his expression grim. Leaning against the wall was Colonel Farooq Siddiqui, head of the ISI's Special Projects Division, his arms crossed, his eyes intense.

"The Indians have made their move," Khan said finally, breaking the heavy silence. His voice was low, measured. "We cannot afford to be left behind."

General Javed nodded slowly, his jaw set. "We need a deterrent," he replied. "And we need it fast."

Colonel Farooq cleared his throat, his tone calm but firm. "We have the resources, the people, the know-how," he said. "But we will need help—discreet help."

Khan turned to him, his gaze piercing. "You mean the Americans?"

Farooq nodded. "Among others," he replied. "There are those who want to see us succeed, for their reasons."

Khan considered this for a moment, weighing the risks and benefits. Then he nodded. "Do what you must, Colonel," he said. "But remember, this must be done quietly, with absolute discretion. Failure is not an option."

Farooq inclined his head. "Understood, Prime Minister," he replied. "I have just the man in mind."

The Partition: A Legacy of Division

The events unfolding in 1974 were just another chapter in the tumultuous history of South Asia. The seeds of this nuclear race between India and Pakistan had been sown decades earlier, in the dying days of the British Empire.

In 1947, the British hastily withdrew from the Indian subcontinent, leaving behind a nation in chaos. The independence of India and the creation of Pakistan were supposed to mark a new beginning, but instead, they unleashed a storm of violence, displacement, and death.

The partition of British India, a process that divided the land based on religious lines, was one of the largest and bloodiest migrations in human history. Millions of Hindus, Sikhs, and Muslims were uprooted from their homes, forced to flee across newly drawn borders that had been hurriedly sketched by British officials. Families were torn apart, and entire communities were destroyed. The scars of partition ran deep, as trains full of refugees arrived at their destinations bearing the dead and wounded, victims of the religious and ethnic violence that erupted on both sides of the divide.

Over ten million people crossed borders, Muslims fleeing to Pakistan, Hindus and Sikhs fleeing to India. The death toll was staggering estimates range from several hundred thousand to two million dead in just a few short months. The rivers of the Punjab ran red with blood. Amidst this carnage, the nascent states of India and Pakistan were born.

A Cold War Frontier

But the partition was not just a local tragedy—it had global repercussions. As the Cold War deepened, both India and Pakistan found themselves courted by the world's superpowers. The United States, wary of Soviet expansion, saw in Pakistan a key ally in the region, a buffer against communism's spread. India, under Prime Minister Jawaharlal Nehru, chose a path of non-alignment but increasingly leaned toward the Soviet Union, solidifying its place in the Eastern bloc by the 1970s.

Pakistan, under leaders like Field Marshal Ayub Khan and later General Zia-ul-Haq, became a key partner in America's strategy to contain communism. The U.S. provided military aid and economic assistance, building up Pakistan's armed forces in exchange for strategic cooperation. By the 1980s, Pakistan would become a critical player in the covert war against the Soviet occupation of Afghanistan.

Meanwhile, India pursued its own ambitions. Under Indira Gandhi, India sought regional dominance and, after its victory in the 1971 war that resulted in the creation of Bangladesh, India's confidence soared. It wasn't long before India tested its first nuclear device in 1974, sending shockwaves through the region and beyond.

A Race for Survival

In Islamabad, the mood was grim but resolute. India's nuclear test had changed the game. Pakistan, always aware of its smaller size and military inferiority compared to India, now faced an existential threat. Zulfiqar Khan and his generals knew they could not afford to let India maintain a nuclear monopoly.

Thus began Pakistan's quest for the bomb. It was no longer a matter of prestige; it was a matter of survival. Pakistanis still carried the scars of partition and the humiliation of the 1971 war. Now, they were determined to ensure that such a defeat would never happen again.

Prime Minister Zulfiqar Khan, flanked by General Javed and Colonel Farooq, knew that they had to act quickly. The world was teetering on the brink of disaster. The Cold War was raging on every continent, and South Asia had become one of its most volatile frontiers. In the background, the United States and the Soviet Union, both armed to the teeth with nuclear weapons, stood ready to annihilate each other in a moment's notice. The Cuban Missile Crisis of 1962 had shown how close the world had already come to the edge of nuclear Armageddon, and the fear of another crisis loomed large.

But Pakistan's decision to pursue nuclear weapons wasn't just about India. It was about carving out its place in a world dominated by superpowers. In a region beset by instability, Pakistan needed to assert itself. And with its deepening ties to China and its precarious relationship with the United States, the nuclear bomb became Pakistan's ultimate insurance policy.

Khan turned to Colonel Farooq. "We must succeed where others have failed. This isn't just about balancing India. This is about our survival, our sovereignty."

Farooq nodded. The race had begun, and it was a race that would change the course of history.

Global Reaction

As the world reeled from India's nuclear test, the geopolitical landscape began to shift. In Washington, American officials huddled in dark, smoke-filled rooms, debating their next move. The U.S. had long considered India a counterweight to China, but a nuclear India posed a new challenge. Meanwhile, in Moscow, Soviet leaders worried about the balance of power in South Asia. They had cultivated a close relationship with India, but Pakistan's new ambitions could destabilize the region.

Beijing watched the developments with a mix of alarm and calculation. China had its own rivalry with India, having fought a war with its southern neighbor in 1962. A nuclear India threatened to upset the fragile balance of power in Asia. But a nuclear-armed Pakistan could serve as a useful ally in containing Indian influence.

The stage was set for a new, dangerous chapter in the Cold War—one where South Asia, with its unresolved conflicts, deep-seated mistrust, and historical grievances, would become a flashpoint for nuclear brinkmanship.

Islamabad, Pakistan – The Race Begins

Back in Islamabad, Prime Minister Khan dismissed his advisors after a long meeting. He walked to the window, staring out into the distance. He knew the stakes. He knew what the consequences of failure would be. But he also knew that Pakistan could not afford to be left behind in this nuclear race.

As the door to his office closed behind him, Khan whispered to himself, "For our future."

The shepherd in the Thar Desert, thousands of miles away from these discussions, might never understand the forces that had led to the flash of light that tore through his world. But that blinding flash, that roar from the earth's core, was a

signal to the world that the race had begun.

Chapter 1: The Scientist's Dilemma

Almelo, Netherlands – URENCO Facility

The dull hum of fluorescent lights buzzed overhead as Dr. Kamran Malik sat at his cluttered desk, surrounded by stacks of documents, blueprints, and technical manuals. The sterile, cold glow illuminated the papers sprawled before him, their contents blending into a blur of schematics and equations. His eyes were heavy with exhaustion, the kind that no amount of sleep could remedy. Each day had become an endless loop of calculations and research, but today, there was something different—something ominous that weighed heavily on his mind.

Kamran's fingers absently tapped on the desk as he stared at a sealed telegram resting in the center, an object of dread he had yet to open. He knew the message contained a few simple words, but they carried a weight that could shatter the fragile peace he had built in the Netherlands. The last time he had heard from Colonel Farooq Siddiqui was years ago, back when Kamran had first distanced himself from the political whirlwind of Pakistan. And now, here it was—a direct summons, drawing him back into a world he thought he had left behind.

His mind wandered to his time in Pakistan, to the late nights spent in shadowy rooms, the secret conversations filled with veiled threats and dangerous promises. He had walked away from all of that. Or at least, he had tried. But could one ever truly walk away? The question gnawed at him. Kamran had built a life here, far from the turmoil of home. His career as a physicist had given him the stability he had craved for so long. Yet, the telegram threatened to tear it all apart.

The past had come for him.

He reached for the telegram, his hand shaking slightly. He paused, taking a deep breath before tearing it open. As expected, the message was brief and to the point: "Meet me in Amsterdam. Urgent. – F.S."

Kamran closed his eyes, his mind racing. Farooq Siddiqui was not a man to be ignored. A rising star in Pakistan's intelligence apparatus,

Farooq had a way of getting what he wanted, often by any means necessary. Kamran had been a key figure in the early stages of Pakistan's nuclear research program. Though his work had been technical, detached from the politics of it all, he knew too much. Farooq would use that to reel him back in, and Kamran feared he might not have a choice.

He stood up abruptly, gathering his things. His heart was pounding now, the familiar rhythm of anxiety. As he moved down the corridor of the URENCO facility, the sound of his footsteps echoed, unnervingly loud in the sterile, empty hallway. A few colleagues passed by, their curious glances grazing over him. He could sense their suspicion, the way their eyes lingered a moment too long.

He had felt this before—that gnawing paranoia, the sense of being watched.

Kamran quickened his pace, pushing through the facility's exit doors. The cold Dutch wind hit his face as he stepped outside, a reminder of how far he had come from the dusty streets of Islamabad. He should have felt safe here, in this foreign land, away from the power plays and political machinations. But that illusion had shattered the moment he received the telegram.

Amsterdam, Netherlands – Later That Day

The rain fell steadily as Kamran navigated the cobblestone streets of Amsterdam, the damp air carrying a chill that seeped into his bones. He pulled his coat tighter around himself as he approached Café de Jaren, the meeting spot Farooq had chosen. The café, perched on the banks of the Amstel River, was a popular spot, its warm glow spilling out onto the wet pavement, inviting in patrons seeking refuge from the cold.

Kamran hesitated before stepping inside, taking a moment to survey the bustling interior. The low hum of conversation filled the room, mingling with the soft clinking of glasses and the shuffle of waitstaff. A place like this offered anonymity in its crowds, yet Kamran felt anything but anonymous. His nerves were frayed, and his heart thudded in his chest as he spotted Farooq Siddiqui seated at a small table near the back, partially obscured by a newspaper he held at a calculated angle.

Kamran approached cautiously, his pulse quickening with every step. The room seemed to close in around him as he sat down across from the man who had once held such sway over his life.

"Colonel," Kamran greeted, keeping his voice steady.

Farooq folded the newspaper with deliberate precision, a small smile playing at his lips. He looked just as Kamran remembered—tall, sharp-eyed, his presence both commanding and unsettling. "Kamran," Farooq said, his tone smooth, almost friendly, but with an edge of something darker beneath. "It's been too long."

Kamran nodded, his jaw tight. "What's this about?"

Farooq's smile faded slightly as he leaned forward, lowering his voice. "India," he said simply, the weight of the word hanging in the air between them. "They've tested a nuclear device. We need to respond."

Kamran felt a cold knot form in his stomach. He had seen the headlines earlier that morning—India Tests Nuclear Device; Pakistan on High Alert. The implications were staggering, but hearing the words spoken aloud brought the reality crashing down around him.

"And you want my help," Kamran said, though it was less of a question and more of an acknowledgment of the inevitable.

Farooq nodded, his expression serious now. "Your expertise. Your contacts. We need to move quickly, and we need discretion. The stakes are too high."

Kamran's mind raced, his heart pounding in his chest. He had tried so hard to leave that world behind, to build something here in Europe, far from the political maneuverings of his homeland. But now, it seemed, that world had come for him, whether he liked it or not.

"What makes you think I'll agree?" Kamran asked, his voice low, challenging.

Farooq's eyes narrowed slightly, his smile returning, though it didn't reach his eyes. "Because you know what's at stake. For Pakistan. For your family. You've always been a patriot, Kamran. I'm just reminding you of that."

The words hit harder than Kamran had expected. His family. His mind flashed to thoughts of Amina, his wife, and their two young daughters, still in Pakistan. They were the reason he had left, the reason he had distanced himself from all of this. But Farooq's unspoken threat was clear: if Kamran didn't cooperate, his family might pay the price.

Kamran clenched his fists beneath the table, feeling the weight of the decision pressing down on him. He was trapped. Farooq knew it, and Kamran knew it too.

He took a deep breath, meeting Farooq's gaze. "What do you need?" he asked finally, his voice barely above a whisper.

"Everything," Farooq replied without hesitation. "We need everything."

Chapter 2: The Network Begins

Islamabad, Pakistan – ISI Headquarters

The walls of Colonel Farooq Siddiqui's office were covered with maps, charts, and classified reports—layers of secrets that no one but the ISI's top brass would ever see. The room smelled faintly of cigarette smoke, even though the Colonel hadn't touched one in hours. It was an ingrained habit now—the smell of smoldering tobacco and old paper accompanying him in every tense meeting and clandestine operation he had overseen for Pakistan's intelligence services.

Behind his desk, Farooq sat deep in thought, his eyes scanning the list of names in front of him. Each name represented a possible asset, a piece of the sprawling, delicate network he needed to assemble to secure Pakistan's nuclear ambitions. Yet even in his calm, calculated manner, he could feel the rising pressure from all sides. The Indians had made their move. The world was watching. The clock was ticking.

A knock on the door broke the silence. It was a sharp, familiar sound—his aide, a young officer, entered the room holding a sealed envelope. The ISI insignia stamped on it glistened faintly under the overhead light. Farooq took the envelope and tore it open with the practiced precision of a man who had seen too many classified messages.

He scanned the brief note, his lips curling into a small, satisfied smile. It was from an old contact in the CIA's Islamabad office—John Harrison, a man who owed Farooq more than a few favors. The Americans, it seemed, were willing to look the other way on certain activities. They needed Pakistan as a Cold War ally, especially with the Soviets breathing down their necks in Afghanistan. It was just the kind of subtle encouragement Farooq needed to push his plans forward without too much external interference.

"Good," Farooq murmured under his breath as he set the note aside.

He picked up the phone and dialed a number he knew by heart. "Get me Aziz Khan," he said in a low, controlled tone. "We have a new assignment for him."

Medellín, Colombia – South American Connection

Carlos Rojas was not a man to be trifled with. The Colombian cartel leader lounged in a plush armchair inside his sprawling, opulent mansion, his fingers idly rolling a Cuban cigar between them. Around him, his lieutenants sat in a semicircle, each man brimming with barely contained violence, their loyalty to Rojas unquestionable. The air was thick with the scent of expensive tobacco and the low hum of salsa music drifting through the mansion's hallways.

Seated across from Rojas was Aziz Khan, the Pakistani intermediary sent by Kamran Malik and Farooq Siddiqui to secure a crucial deal. Khan was calm, composed, his gaze steady as he looked across the room at Rojas, who took a long, deliberate puff of his cigar before speaking.

"Señor Khan," Rojas began, his voice smooth but dangerous, "you come to me for uranium. A risky request, no? Why should I help you with such... delicate matters?"

Aziz's smile was barely perceptible, but his calm demeanor never wavered. "Because, Señor Rojas," he replied, his voice steady, "you and I both understand the value of power. And power comes not only from money, but from alliances. You help us now, and we both gain something far more valuable than currency."

Rojas chuckled softly, the sound filled with both amusement and menace. "You are bold, Khan. I like that. But remember," he added, leaning forward, his voice dropping to a near whisper, "this business is not for the faint-hearted. One wrong move, and you disappear."

Aziz nodded, unfazed by the threat. "I understand, Señor Rojas. We are prepared to pay handsomely for your assistance."

The tension in the room was thick, but the two men understood each other. The stakes were high, and neither could afford to make a mistake.

Rojas took another long drag from his cigar, letting the smoke curl lazily in the air. He studied Khan for a moment longer before nodding slowly. "Very well," he said, his voice smooth as silk. "I will help you. But if you cross me..."

Aziz gave a small nod of acknowledgment. "We have no intention of crossing you," he said, his tone final.

With the deal sealed, both men knew they had entered into a dangerous new game—one that could either elevate them to new heights or destroy them completely. But in this business, calculated risks were the only way forward.

Paris, France – The Scientific Conference

The grand conference hall in Paris buzzed with the low murmur of conversation as some of the world's most prominent physicists and scientists mingled, exchanging ideas, theories, and pleasantries. The room, a stunning blend of art and intellect, was filled with elegant chandeliers and intricate frescoes, lending an air of refinement to the gathering.

Dr. Kamran Malik moved quietly through the crowd, his eyes scanning the faces around him. He had attended conferences like this many times, but tonight, his mind was elsewhere—focused on the mission that now consumed his life.

He spotted Dr. Safia Khan standing near one of the large windows that overlooked the city. Her expression was distant, her gaze fixed on the twinkling lights of Paris. Kamran approached her slowly, his mind racing. He had known Safia for years, admired her brilliance, but he wasn't sure how she would react to what he was about to propose.

"Dr. Khan," Kamran greeted her with a warm smile, his voice breaking through her thoughts.

Safia turned, her eyes narrowing slightly in surprise. "Dr. Malik," she replied coolly. "I didn't expect to see you here."

Kamran chuckled softly, though there was little humor in the sound. "I suppose that's true for both of us," he said. "What brings you to Paris?"

Safia's expression remained guarded, her eyes studying Kamran as if searching for hidden motives. "The same thing that brings all of us here—science, discovery... perhaps a little politics," she said, her tone measured.

Kamran's smile faded slightly. "Politics? I didn't think you were one to mix science and politics, Safia."

She raised an eyebrow. "And I didn't think you were the type to mix with people like Colonel Siddiqui," she replied, her voice sharp, cutting through the polite façade.

Kamran's heart skipped a beat, but he didn't let his composure slip. "Sometimes, we don't have a choice," he said softly. "Safia, we need to talk. Privately."

She hesitated for a moment, her instincts telling her to walk away. But something in Kamran's tone—something in the way he said her name—gave her pause. She glanced around the room before nodding. "Alright," she said quietly. "Let's go."

They slipped away from the crowd, finding a small alcove away from prying eyes. The tension between them was palpable.

"What's going on, Kamran?" Safia asked, her voice firm but filled with concern.

Kamran didn't waste time. "I'm here on behalf of our country," he said. "We need your help. This is bigger than either of us."

Safia crossed her arms, her expression hardening. "And if I say no?" she asked, her voice laced with skepticism.

Kamran met her gaze, his voice filled with quiet intensity. "Then you walk away, and we find someone else. But Safia, you know what's at stake. You know what will happen if we don't act."

Her eyes flickered with emotion—fear, anger, doubt—all mixed together. She looked away, taking a deep breath. "What do you need?" she asked quietly.

"Your expertise," Kamran replied. "Your contacts. Your loyalty."

Safia was silent for a long moment, weighing her options. Finally, she spoke, her voice barely above a whisper. "And what's in it for me, Kamran? What do I gain from all of this?"

Kamran hesitated, his heart pounding. "A chance to do something that matters. A chance to protect our country."

Safia turned to face him fully, her expression softening slightly. "Alright," she said after a long pause. "I'm in. But don't make me regret this."

Kamran smiled, though there was a hint of sadness in his eyes. He knew what he was asking of her, and he knew the cost would be high. But he also knew they had no other choice.

Cairo, Egypt – Secret Meeting with Libyan Envoys

In the dimly lit room of an old Cairo hotel, Kamran sat across from two stern-faced Libyan envoys sent by Colonel Gaddafi. The air was thick with tension, the sound of the bustling city outside a stark contrast to the quiet intensity within the room.

The taller of the two envoys spoke first, his voice cold and clipped. "Colonel Gaddafi is prepared to offer uranium from Mali and funding, in exchange for nuclear expertise."

Kamran nodded, keeping his expression neutral. "And what does he want in return?"

The shorter envoy leaned forward, his voice dropping to a whisper. "He wants the knowledge and the capability to build his own bomb."

Kamran's heart skipped a beat. He had suspected as much, but hearing the words spoken aloud made the reality all the more dangerous. "That's a big ask," he said slowly. "And a dangerous one."

The taller envoy's lips curled into a thin smile. "Dangerous? Perhaps. But the rewards... the power it brings... are worth the risk."

Kamran remained silent for a moment, his mind racing. He knew the stakes. He knew the consequences of what he was about to agree to. But there was no turning back now.

"We'll need to discuss the terms," Kamran said finally, his voice steady.

The two envoys exchanged a glance before nodding. "Agreed," the taller one said.

Chapter 3: Recruiting the Team

Dubai, UAE – Sheikh Khalid's Penthouse Suite

The penthouse suite of Sheikh Khalid al-Fahd was a world of opulence, with its marble floors, intricately carved wooden furniture, and floor-to-ceiling windows that offered a breathtaking view of the glittering city below. The Sheikh, dressed in a tailored white kandura, sat behind a massive mahogany desk, his fingers lightly drumming on the surface. His dark, calculating eyes locked onto Dr. Kamran Malik, who stood across from him, his demeanor composed, but inside, he was acutely aware of the stakes of this meeting.

"Sheikh Khalid," Kamran began, choosing his words carefully, "we need secure routes, funding, and protection from international scrutiny. You have the influence to make this happen."

Sheikh Khalid leaned back in his chair; his face expressionless as he contemplated the request. His hands steepled in front of him, a faint smile playing at his lips. "And in return?" he asked, his voice carrying the faintest trace of a Western education layered beneath the melodic Arabic cadence.

Kamran had anticipated this question. The Sheikh was not a man to be easily persuaded. "In return, Pakistan's nuclear capabilities will be available to the Arab world if the need arises. You'll have the assurance that your interests in the region are protected, both from external threats and internal instability."

The Sheikh studied Kamran carefully, his gaze unflinching. "You ask much," he said slowly, his tone one of quiet calculation. "You must understand, I have many investments, many interests across the globe. And yet, nuclear capability... that is something which attracts the wrong kind of attention."

Kamran didn't flinch. "With respect, Sheikh Khalid, your influence has already attracted attention. But imagine how much more secure you would be with Pakistan standing behind you, with the ability to deter any threat. Your enemies will think twice before challenging you."

The Sheikh's smile widened slightly, but his eyes remained cold. "Very well," he said after a long pause. "But understand this: I will expect full transparency on all developments. I will not be kept in the dark."

Kamran nodded. "Of course. This is a partnership. We will keep you informed every step of the way."

The Sheikh inclined his head slightly, a gesture of agreement, but Kamran could sense the layers of mistrust beneath the surface. This was a man who would always be watching, always be waiting for the slightest hint of betrayal.

"As a token of good faith," the Sheikh continued, "I will arrange for the safe passage of your shipments through Dubai's free ports. I will also ensure that no one interferes with your movements. But remember, Dr. Malik, if you cross me, you will wish you had never set foot in this city."

Kamran gave a curt nod. "You have my word, Sheikh Khalid."

With that, the meeting was concluded. Kamran left the penthouse with a mixture of relief and wariness. He had secured the Sheikh's support, but he knew that this alliance was fraught with danger. Trust was a fragile commodity in this world, and it could be shattered in an instant.

Zurich, Switzerland – The Broker's Dilemma

In a high-rise suite overlooking the tranquil shores of Lake Zurich, The Broker sat in quiet contemplation, swirling a glass of scotch in his hand. His world was one of shadows, where deals were made and broken in the dead of night, and where alliances shifted like the wind. Tonight, however, the weight of his decisions pressed heavily on his mind.

On the sleek wooden table before him lay a series of reports—intelligence gathered from multiple sources, each one a puzzle piece in the intricate web of smuggling, trade, and subterfuge that Kamran Malik's network relied on. The Broker had been facilitating the movement of goods for months—small, innocuous shipments that would arouse no suspicion, yet collectively, they were critical to Pakistan's nuclear ambitions.

But now, the Russians had reached out. They wanted him to betray Malik's network. The coded message had been clear: provide information about the uranium shipments, or risk his family's safety. It was a line The Broker had walked for years, balancing between powerful, ruthless forces. But this time, it felt different. The stakes were higher.

The phone on the table rang, pulling him from his thoughts. He set down his glass and answered, his voice calm and measured. "It's me."

"Do we have a deal?" the voice on the other end, thick with a Russian accent, asked.

The Broker hesitated for a moment, his mind racing. "The shipment is moving through Hong Kong," he said finally, choosing his words carefully. "But I'll need more time to confirm the exact details."

"Make sure you do," the Russian replied. "Or you know what will happen."

The line went dead, and The Broker set the phone down, a knot of tension tightening in his chest. He was playing a dangerous game—balancing his loyalty to Kamran Malik while trying to placate the Russians. But he knew one thing: if either side suspected he was double-crossing them, he would be dead.

He stood and walked to the window, staring out at the lights of the city reflected in the lake below. He had survived this long by staying one step ahead, by seeing the moves on the chessboard before anyone else. Now, he just had to stay alive long enough to make his next move.

Hong Kong – Zhao Li's Office

The scent of incense and the low hum of traditional Chinese music filled the air in Zhao Li's office, a stark contrast to the ruthless world of organized crime that Zhao commanded. His office, located on the top floor of a nondescript building in Kowloon, was an oasis of calm amidst the chaos of the city below.

Zhao sat behind his desk, his sharp, calculating eyes fixed on Kamran Malik, who stood before him. Kamran had come to Hong Kong to finalize arrangements for the movement of crucial components for Pakistan's nuclear program through the city's ports. Zhao's Triad organization controlled these routes, and without his help, Kamran's shipments would never make it out of the country.

"There are whispers in the streets," Zhao said, his voice smooth but edged with menace. "The Americans are watching. They suspect something."

Kamran's expression remained calm, though inside, he felt a flicker of unease. "They've suspected for years," he replied. "But they have no proof. And if we move carefully, they won't get any."

Zhao studied Kamran for a long moment, his fingers tapping lightly on the desk. "You're asking a great deal of me," he said. "My organization takes great risks by moving your materials. And if I sense even the slightest hint of betrayal, I will not hesitate to act."

Kamran nodded. "I understand. But we're in this together. If we succeed, we both benefit. If we fail…"

Zhao's eyes narrowed. "There will be no 'we' if you fail, Dr. Malik. Remember that."

Kamran held Zhao's gaze, his own resolve hardening. "I won't forget."

The deal was struck, but Kamran knew that Zhao's loyalty, like that of many others, was conditional. The Triad leader would not hesitate to turn on him if things went south. But for now, the shipment would move forward, and Kamran's plans would remain intact.

London, UK – The University Corridor

At a prestigious university in London, Dr. Ahmed Qureshi walked through the quiet corridors, his thoughts heavy with the weight of his new mission. He had been recruited to oversee a small but crucial part of the nuclear project—recruiting the brightest minds in nuclear physics, men and women who could work discreetly, far from the prying eyes of Western intelligence agencies.

He spotted a young doctoral student, Ali, hunched over a notebook in the library. Ali was brilliant, a rising star in the field of nuclear physics, and Qureshi knew he was the perfect candidate for the team.

"Ali," Qureshi said softly, approaching the young man. "I need to talk to you."

Ali looked up, his eyes wide with surprise. "Of course, Professor," he said, setting down his pen.

Qureshi led him to a quiet corner of the library, where they could speak privately. "You're talented," Qureshi began, "but talent like yours shouldn't be wasted on theory alone. There's a greater purpose for men like you—something that could change the course of history."

Ali's eyes widened, his curiosity piqued. "What do you mean?"

Qureshi's voice lowered. "There is a project—one that could secure Pakistan's future, protect it from those who would seek to destroy us. We need men like you to make it happen."

Ali hesitated, sensing the gravity of the offer. "What are you asking me to do?" he asked quietly.

Qureshi smiled faintly. "Join us," he said. "Use your talents for something that matters. Help us build something that will ensure our country's safety for generations to come."

Ali took a deep breath, his mind racing. He had always wanted to make a difference, to contribute to something greater than himself. And now, it seemed, he had the opportunity to do just that.

"I'll think about it," Ali said finally.

Qureshi nodded, his expression knowing. "Don't take too long," he said. "The world is changing quickly, and we need men like you now more than ever."

As Qureshi walked away, he knew that Ali would join the team. He had seen the spark of ambition in the young man's eyes, the desire to prove himself. And in this game, ambition was a powerful motivator.

Chapter 4: Shopping

Zurich, Switzerland – The Broker's Dilemma

The Broker stood at the window of his luxurious suite, his fingers tapping rhythmically against the cool glass. Below him, the city of Zurich hummed with quiet efficiency, its streets orderly, its people purposeful. But for The Broker, tonight was different. Tonight, the calm exterior of this financial metropolis felt like a veneer, a facade that could shatter at any moment.

On his desk lay a series of reports, shipments being routed from Hong Kong through various free trade zones, parts and materials that would never raise suspicion on their own but were essential to the construction of Pakistan's uranium enrichment program. Each shipment was carefully logged, each step of the process meticulously orchestrated to avoid the scrutiny of international regulators.

But tonight, there was another problem. His Russian contact had grown impatient. They wanted more information about Kamran Malik's network, and they wanted it fast.

The phone on the desk rang, its shrill sound slicing through the silence. The Broker answered, his voice steady, though his mind was racing.

"It's Rojas," came the gruff voice of Carlos Rojas, the South American cartel leader The Broker had recently begun dealing with. "We have a situation."

The Broker's heart sank. "What kind of situation?" he asked, his voice calm, though a bead of sweat trickled down the back of his neck.

"One of my shipments didn't make it through Hong Kong," Rojas replied. "I suspect someone's been talking to the Americans. I don't like being played."

The Broker closed his eyes, taking a deep breath. He couldn't afford to lose Rojas as an ally, not now. "I'll look into it," he promised. "But you need to stay calm. If you start making noise, it will draw attention."

"""

Rojas growled on the other end of the line. "You better fix this, amigo. If I find out you've double-crossed me, you'll wish you hadn't."

The line went dead, and The Broker set the phone down, his heart pounding in his chest. He knew he was walking a tightrope, balancing between Kamran's network, the Russians, and now the South Americans. One wrong move, and it could all come crashing down.

He poured himself a drink, the amber liquid swirling in the glass, and stared out the window at the glittering city below. He had survived this long by staying ahead of the game, by anticipating every move. But tonight, the stakes felt higher than ever.

Hong Kong – Zhao Li's Warehouse

Zhao Li stood in the dimly lit warehouse, the faint scent of oil and metal filling the air. Stacks of wooden crates lined the walls, each one marked with codes that would mean little to the untrained eye but held the secrets to Pakistan's nuclear ambitions. The parts inside these crates were small—valves, pipes, specialized metals—but when assembled, they would form the heart of the centrifuges needed to enrich uranium.

Kamran Malik stood beside him, his eyes scanning the room. "Everything's here?" he asked.

Zhao nodded, his expression calm but guarded. "Everything you need, Dr. Malik. But moving it out of Hong Kong won't be easy. The Americans are watching."

Kamran frowned, his mind working through the logistics. "We'll need to split the shipment," he said. "Move the parts through different ports, different routes. They can't track everything."

Zhao's lips curled into a thin smile. "That's what I do best. But it will cost you."

Kamran nodded, expecting as much. "We'll make sure you're compensated. But this needs to be done quietly."

Zhao's smile widened. "Quiet is my specialty, Dr. Malik. You'll have your shipment."

Kamran studied Zhao for a moment, sensing the layers of mistrust beneath the man's calm exterior. But he also knew that Zhao was a professional, a man who knew how to get things done. For now, their alliance was holding, but Kamran knew better than to let his guard down.

As Kamran turned to leave, Zhao's voice stopped him. "One more thing," Zhao said, his tone shifting slightly. "There's been talk in the streets—rumors about your network, about leaks. I've kept my ears open, but I thought you should know."

Kamran's eyes narrowed. "Who's talking?"

Zhao shrugged. "That's the problem. It's not just one source. The Americans are looking for something, and they're willing to pay for information. Be careful, Dr. Malik. You have many friends, but just as many enemies."

Kamran nodded, feeling the weight of Zhao's warning settle in his chest. He knew the risks, but hearing it confirmed only heightened his sense of urgency.

Zurich, Switzerland – The Banker's Visit

The Broker's fingers tapped rhythmically on the polished wood of his desk as he waited for his next visitor. The air in his suite felt heavy, the weight of his decisions pressing down on him. He knew that tonight's meeting would be critical. The Bank of Credit and Commerce International (BCCI) had been instrumental in moving funds for Kamran Malik's network, and the man he was about to meet controlled the flow of money that kept the entire operation running smoothly.

A knock at the door signaled the arrival of his guest. The Broker opened it to reveal Mr. Khan, a middle-aged Pakistani banker with sharp, calculating eyes and a slight smile that never quite reached his lips.

"Mr. Khan," The Broker greeted, extending his hand.

"Good to see you again," Khan replied, shaking his hand firmly before stepping inside.

The two men sat across from each other at the desk, the tension in the room palpable. Khan was one of the few people The Broker trusted—if trust was even possible in this business. But even with Khan, there were limits.

"We need to accelerate the transfers," The Broker said, cutting straight to the point. "Kamran's network is growing, and the Americans are getting too close for comfort."

Khan nodded, his expression thoughtful. "We can move the funds through the usual channels," he said, "but we'll need to be more discreet. The scrutiny on the BCCI has been increasing, and I don't want any unnecessary attention."

The Broker sighed, leaning back in his chair. "We can't afford any delays, Khan. If the money doesn't move, the shipments don't move. And if the shipments don't move..."

Khan raised a hand, stopping him. "I understand," he said calmly. "I'll make sure everything goes through, but we need to be careful. One misstep, and we're both finished."

The Broker nodded, knowing that Khan was right. The margins were razor-thin, and the slightest error could bring everything crashing down. But for now, they were still in the game, and that was all that mattered.

Ankara, Turkey – The Financier's Deal

In a smoke-filled room deep within the bustling markets of Ankara, a man known only as The Financier sat across from a Turkish businessman. The room was cluttered with papers, ledgers, and maps, each one detailing the movement of funds, materials, and people across borders, all connected to Kamran Malik's growing operation.

The Financier had been orchestrating the movement of money through the Hundi and Hawala networks, using centuries-old methods to ensure that no trace of the transactions could be found. He was a master at making money disappear, and tonight, he was finalizing another critical deal.

"The funds will move from Zurich to Dubai, then onto Karachi," The Financier explained, his voice calm and measured. "No one will see it coming. The transfers will be small, routed through dozens of accounts. By the time it reaches its destination, it will be untraceable."

The Turkish businessman, a heavyset man with a thick mustache and shrewd eyes, nodded in approval. "Good," he said. "The last shipment went smoothly. Let's keep it that way."

The Financier smiled faintly. "I always deliver."

As the two men shook hands, The Financier knew that the next phase of Kamran Malik's plan was now in motion. The money was flowing, the shipments were moving, and the game was on.

Chapter 5: The Smuggling Ring

Hong Kong – Remote Warehouse

The dim light from a single bulb barely illuminated the large, dusty warehouse on the outskirts of Hong Kong. Stacks of wooden crates lined the walls, some marked with codes, others unmarked, their contents a mystery to the untrained eye. The air was thick with the scent of oil and metal, the quiet hum of the city's industrial zone faint in the distance. Kamran Malik stood in the center of the room, his eyes scanning the surroundings, his posture calm but alert.

Zhao Li, the Triad leader with whom Kamran had formed a tenuous alliance, stepped out of the shadows, his face partially obscured by the dim light. Flanked by two of his men, Zhao had the air of a man who was both calculating and dangerous—a man who knew exactly how much power he held.

Kamran nodded in acknowledgment. "Is everything ready?" he asked, his voice low and steady.

Zhao smiled faintly, his hands clasped behind his back. "The shipments are prepared, Dr. Malik. But as always, we must be cautious. The Americans are watching, and my sources tell me they've been asking questions in the port."

Kamran's expression remained unchanged, though his mind raced with the implications. He had anticipated this. "We'll use the decoy routes," he said. "Split the shipment, send half through the port in Ho Chi Minh City and the other half through Taiwan. They won't be able to track everything."

Zhao's smile widened, his dark eyes gleaming in the dim light. "You're a careful man, Malik. I like that. But remember—every move we make adds risk. And if something goes wrong, I won't be the one to take the fall."

Kamran met Zhao's gaze, unflinching. "Neither will I," he replied. "That's why we need to make sure nothing goes wrong."

For a moment, the two men stood in silence, the weight of their unspoken agreement hanging in the air. Both understood the stakes, and both knew that trust was a luxury neither could afford.

"Very well," Zhao said finally. "My men will handle the shipments. The parts will be in Karachi within a week."

Kamran nodded, satisfied for now. "Good. Let me know if anything changes."

Zhao inclined his head slightly, then turned and disappeared into the shadows, leaving Kamran alone in the warehouse. Kamran stood there for a moment longer, his mind running through the logistics, the contingencies. He knew that Zhao was right—each step they took brought them closer to the edge. But Kamran also knew that there was no turning back now.

Karachi, Pakistan – The Safe House

The safe house in Karachi was a modest, unremarkable building tucked away in a quiet neighborhood. From the outside, it looked no different from any other house in the area—faded paint, a rusty gate, and windows that were always closed. But inside, it was a hub of activity.

Kamran sat at a small wooden table, poring over documents and maps, his mind focused on the details of the operation. His second-in-command, Arif, stood by the window, watching the street below with quiet vigilance.

"We've confirmed the shipment routes," Arif said, not taking his eyes off the street. "Everything's moving as planned. But Zhao's right—the Americans are getting too close. We've had a few close calls."

Kamran nodded, his gaze still on the documents. "We'll need to change our routes again after this shipment. They can't track what they can't predict."

Arif turned to face him, a flicker of concern in his eyes. "How long can we keep this up?"

Kamran set down the papers and leaned back in his chair, his expression thoughtful. "As long as we have to," he replied. "But we'll need to accelerate the timeline. Once the parts are in place, we can move forward with the next phase."

Arif crossed his arms, leaning against the wall. "What about The Broker? Can we still trust him?"

Kamran's expression hardened slightly. "We have no choice. He's too valuable, and he knows too much. But we'll keep an eye on him."

Arif nodded, understanding the unspoken implication. In this game, trust was fleeting, and loyalty could shift with the wind.

Zurich, Switzerland – The Broker's Suite

The Broker sat at his desk, staring at the encrypted message on his screen. It had come through one of his secure channels, a simple directive: "The Americans are closing in. Prepare for contingencies."

He sighed, rubbing his temples. The pressure was mounting from all sides—the Russians were growing impatient, the South Americans were making demands, and now the Americans were closing in on Kamran Malik's operation. Every day, the stakes grew higher, and The Broker knew that one misstep could cost him everything.

He reached for the phone and dialed a number. After a few rings, a voice answered on the other end.

"It's me," The Broker said. "We have a problem."

The voice on the other end was calm but direct. "What kind of problem?"

"The Americans are getting too close. We need to divert them—throw them off the scent."

There was a pause, then the voice replied. "I'll take care of it. But be careful. If they catch wind of what we're doing..."

The Broker nodded, though the person on the other end couldn't see him. "I know. Just make sure it's done."

He hung up the phone and leaned back in his chair, his mind racing. He knew he had to stay ahead of the game, to anticipate every move. But the walls were closing in, and he could feel the pressure tightening around him.

Dubai, UAE – The Shipping Hub

In the bustling port of Dubai, crates marked with innocuous labels were being loaded onto a cargo ship bound for Karachi. The port workers moved quickly, oblivious to the true nature of the shipment they were handling. For them, it was just another day's work, moving goods from one place to another.

But for Kamran Malik, this shipment was everything. Inside the crates were the final pieces of the puzzle—parts that would bring Pakistan one step closer to its nuclear ambitions. Kamran had taken every precaution, using multiple front companies, false manifests, and decoy shipments to ensure that the Americans would never find out what was really being moved.

As the cargo ship set sail, disappearing onto the horizon, Kamran allowed himself a brief moment of relief. The pieces were moving into place, and soon, everything would be ready.

Chapter 6: The Intermediary

Zurich, Switzerland – The Broker's Suite

The Broker sat behind his massive oak desk, the soft glow of his desk lamp casting shadows across the luxurious suite. The faint sound of classical music played from the speakers in the background, a stark contrast to the storm of chaos brewing outside his carefully curated world. He poured himself a glass of whiskey, the ice clinking softly as it hit the glass. His mind was racing, calculating his next move in the ever-complicated web he found himself entangled in.

The encrypted messages from Kamran and the others had grown more frequent, and more urgent. The Americans were closing in, and the Russians were growing restless. Everyone had their own agenda, and The Broker had to keep juggling these fragile alliances.

He leaned back in his leather chair, picking up the phone and dialing a number. After a few rings, a gruff voice answered.

"It's time to move the funds," The Broker said, his voice smooth, controlled. "We need the channels open by tomorrow. No delays."

The voice on the other end grunted in acknowledgment. "We'll have it ready. But you know the Americans are looking into everything now. It won't be as easy as before."

The Broker's lips curled into a faint smile. "It's never easy. But that's what we're paid for."

He hung up the phone and took a sip of whiskey, savoring the warmth as it spread through his chest. He knew that the money had to keep flowing, that the smuggling routes had to remain open, and that every transaction had to be invisible. The Americans were watching, but The Broker prided himself on his ability to stay one step ahead. For now, at least.

Karachi, Pakistan – The Intermediary

In a small, dimly lit office in Karachi, Javed Akhtar was quietly making his rounds. The intermediary between the various operatives involved in Kamran's grand plan, Javed was a man who knew how to move in the shadows. His fingers danced over the keys of an encrypted laptop as he sent instructions to contacts in Dubai, Zurich, and Hong Kong, ensuring that the flow of money, information, and goods remained uninterrupted.

He took a deep breath, glancing at the encrypted message from The Broker. The instructions were clear: the funds would be moved through a series of Hawala networks, routed through Dubai and Ankara, and eventually laundered through front companies in Europe. Javed had been doing this for years, and he knew the stakes. But lately, something felt different—there was more pressure, more scrutiny. The Americans were getting closer, and every day brought new risks.

He finished typing, hitting "send" before leaning back in his chair. The old fan in the corner of the room whirred softly, doing little to ease the suffocating heat. Javed rubbed his temples, feeling the weight of the operation pressing down on him. He knew that he was a small piece in a much larger game, but that didn't make the pressure any less real.

His phone buzzed on the desk, and he glanced at the screen. It was a message from Kamran: Status?

Javed quickly typed a reply. Funds are moving. Everything on schedule.

He set the phone down, exhaling slowly. The funds were in motion, and for now, the plan was intact. But Javed couldn't shake the feeling that something was about to go wrong.

Hong Kong – Zhao Li's Headquarters

Zhao Li sat in his private office, a large room filled with opulent furnishings, antique furniture, and priceless artwork. The air smelled faintly of incense, a calming contrast to the intensity of the conversation unfolding before him. Across from the desk sat his niece, Mai Ling, her face serious, her eyes sharp as she listened to her uncle's instructions.

"There's a problem with the Americans," Zhao said, his voice calm but laced with authority. "They've been poking around in the port, asking too many questions. We need to make sure the next shipment goes through without issue."

Mai Ling nodded. "I've already taken care of it," she replied. "The decoy shipment is being prepped. The real cargo will be rerouted through Macau, then sent to Karachi. The Americans won't know where to look."

Zhao smiled faintly, proud of his niece's quick thinking. She had proven herself time and again, and he trusted her more than anyone else in his organization. "Good," he said. "But keep an eye on them. They're getting desperate."

Mai Ling leaned forward slightly, her voice lowering. "What about Malik? Do you still trust him?"

Zhao's expression darkened. "Malik is useful—for now. But trust? No. We watch him closely. If he becomes a liability, we'll deal with him."

Mai Ling nodded, her face unreadable. She understood the game they were playing, and she knew that in their world, alliances were fragile and temporary. For now, Kamran Malik was an asset, but she knew that could change in an instant.

Dubai, UAE – The Free Trade Zone

The Dubai Free Trade Zone was a bustling hub of commerce, where goods from all over the world moved in and out of the city's ports, their origins and destinations often shrouded in secrecy. It was the perfect place for someone like Kamran to move the sensitive components of his operation, hidden among the thousands of other shipments passing through the port.

Kamran stood on the dock, watching as the containers were loaded onto a cargo ship bound for Karachi. Each container was carefully marked and documented; its true contents disguised by layers of false paperwork. It was a system Kamran had perfected, and one that had served him well—until now.

He glanced at his phone, reading the latest update from Javed. The funds were moving, and the shipment was on schedule. Everything was falling into place. But Kamran couldn't shake the feeling that something was wrong. He had learned long ago to trust his instincts, and right now, they were screaming at him.

He turned to his second-in-command, Arif, who was standing nearby, keeping an eye on the loading process. "Double-check everything," Kamran said quietly. "I don't want any surprises."

Arif nodded, his expression serious. "I've already been through it twice, but I'll go over it again."

Kamran watched as Arif moved off to inspect the containers. His mind was racing, running through the logistics, the risks, the potential threats. He knew that the Americans were closing in, and he knew that The Broker was playing both sides. But for now, he had no choice but to trust that everything would hold together.

As the ship pulled away from the dock, Kamran felt a knot of tension tighten in his chest. The next phase of the operation was underway, but the real challenge was just beginning.

Chapter 7: The Espionage Gamble

London, UK – MI5 Headquarters

The office was dim, the soft hum of computers the only sound that filled the space. Peter Grant sat hunched over a pile of documents, his eyes bloodshot from lack of sleep. Every report he read seemed to confirm his worst fears: the Americans were getting too close, and Pakistan's covert nuclear program was on the brink of being exposed.

Across from him, John Harrison, his counterpart from the CIA, paced the room. The tension between them was palpable. They both knew that their governments were playing a dangerous game, allowing a rogue element within their own agencies to assist Pakistan in its pursuit of nuclear weapons. But now, the delicate balance of power was crumbling.

"John, we're running out of time," Grant muttered, his voice thick with exhaustion. "Every day we sit on this, we risk being exposed. We need to do something."

Harrison stopped pacing, turning to face Grant. "You think I don't know that? We're being squeezed from both sides. If we blow the whistle on this, we risk our entire careers. But if we don't—"

"The whole region could spiral out of control," Grant interrupted. "And we'll be the ones holding the bag."

Harrison ran a hand through his hair, his frustration evident. "Look, there's only one way we can get out of this clean. We need to find out who's at the top of 'The Committee.' They're the ones pulling the strings, feeding false intelligence to both of our governments."

Grant leaned back in his chair, his mind racing. "But how? Everyone's watching us now. We make one wrong move, and we're done."

Harrison sat down across from Grant, lowering his voice. "I've been digging into this for months, and I've found a name—an old contact of mine. He's deep in the shadows, but he knows who's really running the show."

Grant raised an eyebrow. "You trust him?"

Harrison hesitated, then nodded. "As much as you can trust anyone in this business. But we need to move fast. He's paranoid, and if he thinks we're onto him, he'll disappear."

Grant's jaw tightened. "Then let's move."

Islamabad, Pakistan – The Web Tightens

In the cool, darkened room of the ISI headquarters, Colonel Farooq Siddiqui stood before a map, his eyes scanning the various locations marked with red pins. The world was closing in on Pakistan's nuclear ambitions, and Farooq knew that the next few days would determine the success or failure of everything they had worked for.

Kamran Malik entered the room, his face a mask of determination, though the weight of the operation was beginning to show in his eyes. Farooq turned to face him, his expression unreadable.

"We're moving into the final phase," Farooq said calmly. "The Americans are getting too close, and the British are sniffing around as well. We need to accelerate the timeline."

Kamran nodded, already anticipating the shift in strategy. "The shipment is on its way to Karachi. Everything is in place, but we need to be ready for a fight."

Farooq folded his arms, his eyes narrowing slightly. "There's something else. The Americans have a mole in our ranks. I don't know who it is yet, but we need to flush them out before they do any more damage."

Kamran clenched his fists. The thought of a traitor among them made his blood boil. "We'll find them," he said quietly. "And when we do..."

Farooq gave a curt nod. "Good. But be discreet. We can't afford any more missteps."

Kamran turned to leave, but Farooq's voice stopped him at the door. "And Kamran—don't trust anyone. Not even those closest to you."

Kamran didn't respond. He didn't need to. The walls were closing in, and he knew that the only person he could truly rely on was himself.

Dubai, UAE – The Broker's Dilemma

The Broker stood at the window of his penthouse suite, staring out at the glittering skyline of Dubai. His phone buzzed on the table behind him, and he turned to see Kamran's name flash on the screen. He hesitated for a moment before picking it up.

"Kamran," The Broker greeted smoothly, his voice as controlled as ever.

"We need to talk," Kamran said, his tone low and urgent. "There's a mole in the operation."

The Broker raised an eyebrow, though he had already suspected as much. "Interesting. Any idea who?"

"Not yet," Kamran replied, frustration evident in his voice. "But I need you to keep your ears to the ground. If anyone's making moves, I want to know about it."

The Broker leaned back in his chair, considering his options. He knew that Kamran's operation was hanging by a thread, and that the Americans were closing in fast. But there were other players in this game—players who might be willing to pay more for the information The Broker held.

"I'll see what I can do," The Broker said finally. "But be careful, Kamran. You're not the only one looking for answers."

Kamran paused for a moment before responding. "I know. But I'll get there first."

The line went dead, and The Broker set the phone down, a faint smile playing at the corners of his lips. He knew that the next few days would be crucial, and that the right move could make or break him. For now, he would wait and see which way the wind blew.

Karachi, Pakistan – A Game of Shadows

Javed Akhtar moved through the crowded streets of Karachi, blending in with the throngs of people going about their daily lives. He had spent years operating in the shadows, and today was no different. The instructions from Kamran had been clear: monitor the flow of information, find the mole, and report back.

He slipped into a small café, taking a seat at a corner table where he had a clear view of the entrance. His contact would be arriving soon—a low-level operative within the ISI who had access to some of the more sensitive intelligence reports.

Javed ordered tea and waited, his mind working through the possibilities. He knew that the Americans were putting pressure on Pakistan, and that there was a traitor in their midst. But who? And how deep did the betrayal go?

His phone buzzed in his pocket, and he glanced at the message. Delayed. 15 minutes.

Javed frowned, setting the phone down. He couldn't afford delays, not now. The Americans were closing in, and every second counted.

He sipped his tea, his eyes scanning the room. Something felt off, but he couldn't put his finger on it.

Then, out of the corner of his eye, he saw them—two men in suits, sitting at a table near the entrance. They were watching him, their eyes cold and calculating.

Javed's heart skipped a beat. He knew those men. They were CIA.

He quickly typed out a message to Kamran: I've been made. Need extraction now.

He slipped his phone back into his pocket, his mind racing. He had to get out of here, and fast.

Washington, D.C. – A Ticking Clock

Lisa Connor sat at her desk, poring over the latest intelligence reports from Pakistan. Her brow furrowed as she read through the intercepted communications. Something big was happening, and she could feel the pressure building. She glanced at the clock on the wall, knowing that time was running out.

Her phone buzzed, and she picked it up. It was a secure message from Harrison.

We've found something. Meet me at the safe house. 30 minutes.

Connor stood up, grabbing her jacket. She knew that whatever Harrison had found could be the key to unraveling the entire operation. But she also knew that they were playing a dangerous game, and that one wrong move could cost them everything.

As she stepped out into the cold night, her mind was already racing with possibilities. The clock was ticking, and they were running out of time.

Chapter 8: The Dead Man's Strategy

Karachi, Pakistan – ISI Headquarters

Colonel Farooq Siddiqui sat in his office, the smoke from his cigarette curling in lazy spirals toward the ceiling. His fingers tapped absently on the armrest of his chair as he stared at the map spread across his desk. The red pins marking Pakistan's covert nuclear operations were scattered across the globe, each one representing a potential point of failure. The Americans were tightening their grip, and Farooq knew that the network they had built over the years was at risk of collapsing under the weight of foreign pressure and internal treachery.

A knock at the door pulled him from his thoughts. "Enter," he called, his voice steady despite the rising tension in his gut.

Kamran Malik stepped into the room, his face grim, the weight of recent events clearly etched in the lines around his eyes. "Colonel, we need to talk."

Farooq gestured to the chair in front of his desk. "Sit," he said. "I assume this is about the mole."

Kamran nodded; his fists clenched at his sides. "Javed's been made. The Americans are onto him."

Farooq's eyes narrowed. "Is he compromised?"

Kamran shook his head. "He managed to get out, but we can't keep running like this. We need a plan. The Americans are closing in, and we've got a leak. If we don't plug it soon, everything we've built will come crashing down."

Farooq exhaled a long stream of smoke, his mind working quickly. "It's time for the Dead Man's Strategy."

Kamran raised an eyebrow, intrigued but wary. "What's that?"

Farooq leaned forward, his eyes hard. "From this point on, every part of the operation functions independently. No one team knows what the others are doing. Each unit is given its own set of tasks, and they report only to me. If one team is compromised, it won't affect the rest of the network."

Kamran's expression was skeptical. "And what about the mole?"

Farooq stubbed out his cigarette, his voice low and cold. "We'll draw them out. I'll feed false information to a few key people and see where it leaks. Whoever takes the bait will be exposed."

Kamran nodded slowly, considering the plan. It was risky, but they were running out of options. "And if it doesn't work?"

Farooq's lips curled into a grim smile. "Then we burn the entire operation to the ground and start over. But I don't plan on failing."

Dubai, UAE – The Broker's Suite

The Broker sat at his desk, his fingers tapping lightly on the polished wood surface. The room was dimly lit, the curtains drawn tight against the bright Dubai skyline. His phone buzzed, and he glanced at the screen. It was a message from one of his European contacts—a name that had surfaced in Kamran's operation.

He leaned back in his chair, a small smile playing on his lips. The pieces were moving into place, and it was only a matter of time before the entire puzzle came into focus.

His thoughts were interrupted by the buzz of an incoming call. The name on the screen made him pause—Colonel Farooq Siddiqui.

He answered the call, his voice smooth. "Colonel, what can I do for you?"

"I need you to move something for me," Farooq said, his tone calm but carrying an edge. "Something sensitive."

The Broker raised an eyebrow. "And what might that be?"

"I'll send you the details," Farooq replied. "But be discreet. If anyone gets wind of this, it could blow everything."

The Broker leaned forward, intrigued. "Consider it done. But you know my terms."

Farooq's voice was cold. "You'll get your payment. But remember, you're playing a dangerous game, Broker. Don't forget who your friends are."

The line went dead, and The Broker set his phone down, his mind racing. Farooq's request was unusual, and that made it valuable. He knew that whatever the Colonel was moving, it was important. And if it was important to Farooq, it was important to others as well.

He picked up his phone again, typing out a quick message to his contact in Zurich. There's a new shipment. Make sure you're ready.

London, UK – The Spy's Dilemma

John Harrison sat in a quiet pub, nursing a pint of beer as he waited for his contact. The air was thick with the smell of stale smoke and old wood, and the low murmur of conversation filled the room. His phone buzzed on the table, and he glanced at the message. It was from Grant.

MI5 is on high alert. Watch your back.

Harrison frowned, his mind racing. He had suspected for some time that their movements were being monitored, but Grant's message confirmed it. They were being watched, and if they weren't careful, they would be silenced before they could expose "The Committee."

The door to the pub creaked open, and a tall, thin man in a trench coat entered. He scanned the room, his eyes landing on Harrison. The man approached the table, sitting down across from him without a word.

"You're late," Harrison said, his voice low.

The man shrugged. "Careful men make it through the night."

Harrison leaned in closer, his voice a whisper. "Do you have what I need?"

The man nodded, sliding a small envelope across the table. "Everything you asked for. Names, dates, locations. But you didn't hear it from me."

Harrison picked up the envelope, slipping it into his coat pocket. "This is it, then?"

The man's expression was grim. "It's enough to bring them down. But you didn't hear it from me."

Harrison nodded, standing up and slipping out of the pub into the cold London night. He knew that the envelope in his pocket held the key to unraveling the entire operation. But it also made him a target.

Islamabad, Pakistan – The Trap is Set

Kamran stood in the shadow of an old building, the cool night air biting at his skin. His eyes scanned the streets, searching for any sign of movement. The information Farooq had planted was already in circulation, and if the mole took the bait, they would have their answer.

A car pulled up across the street, its headlights dimmed. Kamran tensed, his hand hovering over the concealed pistol in his jacket. The driver stepped out, glancing around before slipping into the building.

Kamran's heart pounded in his chest. This was it—the moment of truth.

He moved quickly and silently, following the man into the building. The corridors were dark, and the sound of footsteps echoed faintly in the distance. Kamran's breath was steady, his senses sharp. He had been trained for moments like this.

The man entered a small room at the end of the hallway, the door creaking shut behind him. Kamran pressed his ear to the door, listening to the muffled conversation inside.

"He bought it," the man said, his voice barely audible. "He thinks we're still on his side."

Kamran's blood ran cold. The mole had revealed themselves, and now he knew who had betrayed them.

He stepped back, his mind racing. He had to act fast, or everything would be lost.

Washington, D.C. – Closing In

Lisa Connor sat at her desk; her eyes glued to the latest intelligence reports coming in from Pakistan. Her fingers hovered over the keyboard, typing out commands as she sifted through encrypted communications.

The pieces were starting to fall into place, and she could feel the pressure building.

Her phone rang, and she answered quickly. "Harrison, what did you find?"

"I've got the names," Harrison replied, his voice tense. "And you're not going to like what you hear."

Connor's heart raced. "Who?"

Harrison paused for a moment before speaking. "Farooq Siddiqui. He's running the whole thing."

Connor exhaled sharply, the weight of the revelation hitting her hard. "That's impossible. He's too high up."

"I know," Harrison said. "But the documents don't lie. He's been pulling the strings from the beginning."

Connor leaned back in her chair, her mind racing. Farooq Siddiqui—the man they had been working with, the man they had trusted—was the mastermind behind Pakistan's nuclear ambitions.

She knew that everything was about to change.

Chapter 9: A Dangerous Betrayal

Vienna, Austria – Safe House

The safe house in Vienna was quiet, a sense of foreboding hanging in the air. Kamran Malik sat at a small wooden table, the dim glow of a single lamp casting shadows across his face. His eyes were fixed on the door, his body tense as he waited for the others to arrive. The recent events in Islamabad had shaken him, and he knew that tonight, everything could change.

One by one, his operatives entered the room—Arif, Khalid, Safia, and a few others who had been part of his inner circle for years. Each of them looked wary, their faces tight with suspicion. They had heard the rumors, felt the rising tension. Something was wrong, and they all knew it.

Kamran stood up, his voice low but commanding. "We have a problem," he began, his eyes scanning the room. "There's a mole among us."

The room fell silent, the weight of his words settling like a heavy fog. The operatives exchanged uneasy glances, their faces betraying their fear. Kamran could see it in their eyes—none of them knew who to trust anymore.

"We've compromised," Kamran continued, his gaze hard. "And if we don't find out who's responsible, everything we've worked for will be destroyed."

Arif, always the pragmatist, leaned forward, his voice steady but tense. "What do you want us to do?"

Kamran's eyes locked onto him. "We're going to set a trap," he said. "I've already fed false information to certain people. Whoever leaks it to the Americans is the mole."

Khalid shifted in his seat, his face pale. "And what happens when we find them?"

Kamran's expression darkened. "We deal with them," he replied coldly.

The tension in the room was palpable, and Kamran could feel the unease growing among his operatives. He knew they were scared, knew that the cracks in their trust were starting to show. But he also knew that he couldn't afford to hesitate.

"From now on, no one moves without my direct orders," Kamran said, his voice sharp. "We stick to the plan, and we watch each other's backs. But if anyone steps out of line..."

He didn't need to finish the sentence. They all knew what he meant.

Vienna, Austria – Later That Night

The safe house was quiet again, the shadows deepening as the night wore on. Kamran sat alone in the small living room, his mind racing. He had put his trust in these people, had fought alongside them for years. But now, he couldn't shake the feeling that one of them had betrayed him.

His thoughts were interrupted by the sound of a door creaking open. He glanced up and saw Safia standing in the doorway, her face pale, her eyes filled with uncertainty.

"Kamran," she said softly, stepping into the room. "Can we talk?"

Kamran gestured for her to sit; his expression guarded. "What is it?"

Safia hesitated, her hands trembling slightly as she sat down across from him. "I need to tell you something," she began, her voice barely above a whisper. "I've been in contact with someone...someone from the outside."

Kamran's heart pounded in his chest, but his face remained impassive. "Who?" he asked, his voice cold.

Safia swallowed hard, her eyes darting to the door as if she were afraid someone might overhear. "An old friend in the U.S.," she admitted. "They reached out to me, offered me a way out."

Kamran's jaw tightened, but he kept his voice steady. "And did you take it?"

Safia shook her head quickly, her eyes wide with fear. "No," she said. "But I thought about it."

Kamran exhaled slowly, his mind racing. He had suspected for some time that Safia might be compromised but hearing it from her own lips made it real. He leaned forward, his gaze piercing. "Why are you telling me this now?"

Safia's voice trembled as she spoke. "Because I don't want to betray you, Kamran. I don't want to be part of this anymore. But I also don't want to die."

Kamran studied her face, searching for any hint of deception. He could see the fear in her eyes, the desperation. She was telling the truth—at least, part of it. But he couldn't be sure if she was holding something back.

"I believe you," Kamran said finally, his tone measured. "But you need to understand something, Safia. If I find out you've been lying to me, if I find out you've told them anything...I won't hesitate."

Safia nodded quickly, her face pale. "I understand," she whispered. "I haven't told them anything. I swear."

Kamran stood up, his expression cold. "Then let's keep it that way."

Vienna, Austria – The Trap is Sprung

The next morning, Kamran's plan was set in motion. He had spread false information through his network, a carefully crafted story about a shipment of uranium moving through Eastern Europe. He knew that if the Americans intercepted the shipment, it would mean only one thing—someone in his inner circle had betrayed him.

Hours passed, and Kamran waited, his tension mounting with every tick of the clock. His phone buzzed, and he glanced at the screen. It was a message from one of his contacts.

The Americans took the bait. They're mobilizing forces in Eastern Europe.

Kamran's heart raced. The trap had worked. Now he just needed to find out who had leaked the information.

He called a meeting with his operatives, his face grim as they gathered in the safe house. "The Americans are moving," he said, his voice cold. "Someone gave them the location of the shipment."

The room was silent, the tension thick. Kamran's eyes scanned the faces of his operatives, watching for any sign of guilt, any flicker of fear. His gaze lingered on Safia, but she kept her head down, her hands folded in her lap.

Kamran took a deep breath, his voice steady. "We know there's a mole among us," he said. "And we're going to find out who."

He turned to Arif, who was standing by the door, his face tight with suspicion. "Run the checks," Kamran ordered. "Go through every communication, every contact. I want to know who's been talking."

Arif nodded, his expression grim. "I'll take care of it."

As the operatives filed out of the room, Kamran felt the weight of betrayal pressing down on him. He had spent years building this network, fighting for a cause he believed in. But now, everything was unraveling, and he didn't know who he could trust.

Vienna, Austria – The Revelation

Hours later, Arif returned, his face pale. "Kamran," he said quietly, his voice strained. "We found something."

Kamran's heart pounded in his chest as he followed Arif to a small office in the back of the safe house. Arif handed him a stack of documents, his expression grim.

Kamran flipped through the papers, his eyes scanning the lines of text. And then he saw it—a coded message, sent from one of his operatives to a known CIA contact.

His stomach dropped as he read the name of the sender.

It was Khalid.

Kamran clenched his fists, his anger rising like a tide. Khalid had been with him from the beginning, had fought alongside him in some of the most dangerous operations. And now he had betrayed them all.

"We need to act," Kamran said, his voice cold. "Before he has a chance to run."

Vienna, Austria – The Confrontation

Kamran found Khalid in one of the back rooms, his face calm as he cleaned his weapon. He looked up as Kamran entered, a faint smile on his lips.

"Kamran," Khalid greeted, his tone casual. "What's going on?"

Kamran didn't respond. He stepped forward, his hand resting on the grip of his pistol. "We know," he said quietly, his voice filled with anger.

Khalid's smile faltered, his eyes narrowing. "What are you talking about?"

"The Americans," Kamran said, his voice cold. "You've been feeding them information."

Khalid stood up, his face hardening. "That's a lie."

Kamran drew his pistol, aiming it at Khalid's chest. "Don't lie to me, Khalid. We found the messages."

For a moment, Khalid's face was unreadable. And then, slowly, a cold smile spread across his lips. "You're smarter than I gave you credit for, Kamran," he said, his voice low. "But it's too late. They're coming for you. For all of us."

Kamran's hand tightened on the pistol, his anger boiling over. "Why?" he demanded. "Why did you betray us?"

Khalid's smile faded, and his eyes darkened. "Because you were never going to win," he said coldly. "And I'm not going down with you."

Kamran's finger tightened on the trigger, but before he could fire, Khalid lunged forward, knocking the gun from his hand. They grappled, the fight quick and brutal, their fists landing with sickening thuds.

Kamran's mind raced as they struggled, his anger fueling every punch. He couldn't let Khalid escape. If he did, everything would be lost.

With a final surge of strength, Kamran slammed Khalid against the wall, pinning him in place. He drew a knife from his belt, pressing it against Khalid's throat.

"This is for everyone you betrayed," Kamran growled, his voice filled with rage.

Khalid's eyes widened, but he didn't beg for mercy. He simply stared at Kamran; his lips curled into a mocking smile.

Kamran didn't hesitate. He drove the knife into Khalid's chest, his breath coming in ragged gasps as Khalid's body slumped to the floor.

It was over.

Chapter 10: The Heist

Eastern Europe – A Safe House Near the Facility

The air in the safe house was heavy with tension as Kamran and his team gathered around a table cluttered with blueprints, maps, and hastily scribbled notes. The dim lighting cast long shadows across their faces, making the already grim atmosphere even more oppressive. The uranium enrichment facility loomed not far from their location, a heavily guarded complex deep within the heart of Eastern Europe.

Kamran stood at the head of the table, his eyes scanning the faces of his operatives. Arif, always stoic, was focused on the map. Hauer, the German physicist they had recruited for his expertise in bypassing security systems, sat nervously at the edge, his fingers tapping on the table. He was crucial to the plan but clearly unnerved by the scale of the operation.

"We don't have time for mistakes," Kamran said, his voice low but firm. "You all know the stakes. We get in, we get the uranium, and we get out. No heroics."

Hauer swallowed hard, his eyes darting between Kamran and the blueprints. "Are you sure about the security system?" he asked, his voice trembling slightly. "I mean, this place is like a fortress."

Kamran locked eyes with him, his tone steady but cold. "You're the one who designed half of those systems, Hauer. If anyone can get us through, it's you."

Hauer nodded quickly, though he didn't look convinced. Kamran didn't care. They didn't have the luxury of second-guessing.

Arif tapped the map, pointing to a specific section. "This is our entry point," he said. "A service tunnel on the east side. It's the least monitored, but we still have to deal with the guards at the checkpoint."

Kamran nodded. "We handle them quietly. No gunfire unless absolutely necessary. We need to be in and out before anyone knows we're there."

The rest of the team murmured in agreement, though Kamran could sense the underlying fear. This wasn't just another operation. This was the culmination of years of planning, a dangerous heist that could change everything—or end it all.

"Gear up," Kamran ordered. "We move in fifteen."

Eastern Europe – The Facility

The uranium enrichment facility loomed in the darkness, a hulking mass of concrete and steel surrounded by high fences and watchtowers. Floodlights swept across the perimeter, casting eerie shadows as Kamran's team approached the service tunnel. They moved in silence, their black clothing blending into the night, their footsteps barely audible against the gravel.

Arif led the way, his eyes scanning the area for any sign of movement. Kamran followed close behind, his senses in high alert. Every sound, every flicker of light made his heart race, but he forced himself to stay focused. They were too close to falter now.

They reached the entrance to the service tunnel, a rusted metal door secured by a keypad. Hauer stepped forward, pulling a small device from his pack. His hands shook slightly as he connected the wires and began working on the lock.

"Come on, Hauer," Kamran whispered, his voice barely audible. "We don't have all night."

Hauer muttered something under his breath, his fingers flying over the keypad. After what felt like an eternity, the lock clicked, and the door swung open with a soft creak.

"We're in," Hauer whispered, relief evident in his voice.

Kamran nodded, motioning for the team to move forward. They entered the tunnel, the air cold and damp, the walls lined with pipes and electrical conduits. The sound of their footsteps echoed faintly, adding to the growing sense of unease.

They moved quickly through the tunnel, reaching the first checkpoint—a small room guarded by two men. Kamran signaled to

Arif, who crept forward, his silenced pistol drawn. In a matter of seconds, both guards were down, their bodies slumped against the wall.

"No alarms," Kamran muttered, glancing at the control panel on the wall. "Good."

They continued deeper into the facility, following the route Hauer had mapped out. The corridors were dimly lit, the faint hum of machinery filling the air. Kamran's mind raced as they approached the main storage area, where the uranium was kept.

"This is it," Hauer whispered as they reached the final door. "The uranium is in the vault just beyond this room. But there's a secondary security system here, one I didn't design. It's...complicated."

Kamran shot him in a hard look. "What do you mean 'complicated'?"

Hauer's face paled. "It's biometric. We need a retinal scan from one of the authorized personnel."

Kamran cursed under his breath. "Is there another way in?"

Hauer shook his head. "Not without triggering every alarm in the facility."

Kamran's mind raced. They didn't have time to find one of the authorized personnel, and they couldn't afford to be caught. He turned to Arif. "Find us someone. Quietly."

Arif nodded and disappeared down the hallway, his footsteps barely a whisper. Kamran waited, his heart pounding in his chest. Every second felt like an eternity, the weight of the mission pressing down on him.

Minutes later, Arif returned, dragging a guard with him. The man's eyes were wide with fear, his hands bound behind his back. "This one's authorized," Arif said, his voice low.

Kamran nodded, motioning for Hauer to proceed. Hauer positioned the guard in front of the scanner, forcing his head toward the retinal scanner. The machine beeped, and the door slid open with a soft hiss.

"We're in," Hauer said, his voice barely audible.

They entered the vault, the air inside cold and sterile. Rows of metal cases lined the walls, each one marked with radioactive warning symbols. Kamran's eyes locked onto the prize—the uranium.

"Move fast," Kamran ordered, grabbing one of the cases. "We don't have much time."

The team moved quickly, loading the uranium into specially designed containers that would shield it from detection. Kamran's mind was a blur of calculations, every second bringing them closer to danger. They needed to get out before anyone noticed the breach.

As they worked, Kamran felt a sudden, sharp tension in the air. Something wasn't right. He turned, his eyes scanning the room, his instincts screaming at him to move.

And then the alarms went off.

Eastern Europe – The Escape

The blaring of the alarms echoed through the facility, the red emergency lights flashing in rapid succession. Kamran's heart raced as he grabbed the last container of uranium, shouting orders to his team.

"Go! Now!"

They sprinted toward the exit, their footsteps pounding against the concrete floor as the sound of boots and shouts filled the air. Guards were mobilizing, and Kamran knew they only had seconds before the facility was locked down.

Arif led the way, his gun drawn as they barreled through the corridors, taking out any guards that stood in their path. Kamran stayed close behind, his mind focused on one thing—getting out alive.

They reached the service tunnel, the alarms still blaring in the distance. Kamran glanced back, his heart pounding in his chest. They had the uranium, but they weren't safe yet.

"Hauer, get the door!" Kamran shouted; his voice barely audible over the alarms.

Hauer scrambled to the door, his hands shaking as he worked on the lock. Kamran could feel the tension rising, the walls closing in around them. He knew the guards were closing in.

Finally, the door swung open, and the team rushed through, sprinting toward the waiting vehicles outside. The cold night air hit Kamran's face like a slap, but he didn't slow down. They piled into the trucks, the engines roaring to life.

"Go, go, go!" Kamran shouted, and the trucks sped off into the night, the facility disappearing in the rearview mirror.

Eastern Europe – The Road to Safety

The trucks rumbled down the narrow road, the tension still thick in the air. Kamran sat in the passenger seat, his eyes scanning the horizon for any sign of pursuit. They had made it out of the facility, but he knew they weren't safe yet.

Arif drove in silence, his hands steady on the wheel. The rest of the team sat in the back, their faces pale, their bodies tense with adrenaline.

"We did it," Hauer muttered from the back, his voice shaky. "We actually did it."

Kamran didn't respond. His mind was already racing ahead, thinking of the next step, the next obstacle they would face. The uranium was secure, but the world would soon know what they had done. The consequences would be enormous.

As they approached the border, Kamran allowed himself a brief moment of relief. They had pulled off the heist, against all odds. But he knew that this was just the beginning. The true test was yet to come.

The trucks crossed into friendly territory, the tension slowly dissipating. Kamran leaned back in his seat, his mind still buzzing with the events of the night. They had done it—but at what cost?

"Get some rest," Kamran said to his team as they pulled into a secure location. "We're not done yet."

As the team disembarked, Kamran stood alone, staring into the darkness. The heist was over, but the mission was far from complete. The uranium was in their hands, but now they had to deliver it.

Kamran took a deep breath, his resolve hardening.

The game was far from over.

Chapter 11: The Web Tightens

Washington, D.C. – A Secret Meeting Room

The room was dimly lit, with thick curtains drawn tightly shut, blocking out any light from the outside world. The air was heavy with tension, the faint smell of polished wood and old leather mingling with the subtle scent of cigar smoke that still lingered from a previous meeting. A heavy oak table dominated the center of the room, around which sat a select group of senior officials from the U.S. State Department, their faces a mix of guarded caution and weary concern.

At the far end of the table sat Sheikh Khalid al-Fahd, a tall, imposing figure dressed in a traditional thobe and keffiyeh, his expression calm but calculating. Beside him were two other Arab sheikhs, their dark eyes glinting with a mixture of anxiety and determination. They had flown in discreetly from the Gulf, arriving under the cover of darkness, their private jet touching down at an obscure airfield outside of Washington. This meeting had been arranged with utmost secrecy, and for good reason. They were here to protect their interests—and those of Pakistan.

Sheikh Khalid leaned forward, his hands clasped together, his voice measured but firm. "We need Pakistan as a counterbalance," he began, his accent softened by years of education in the West but still tinged with the distinct cadence of his homeland. "And you need our oil. It's simple."

His statement hung in the air like a challenge. The U.S. officials exchanged uneasy glances. They knew that the sheikhs had a point, but they also knew the risks involved. Pakistan's nuclear ambitions had been a source of growing concern, and the recent developments had only escalated tensions further. But the Arab world's influence—its control over the flow of oil—gave them significant leverage.

Undersecretary Michael Dean, a seasoned diplomat with a reputation for his pragmatism, cleared his throat. "We understand your concerns, Sheikh Khalid," he replied cautiously. "But this is a delicate matter. If we openly support Pakistan's efforts, we risk undermining our alliances with India and other regional players. The political fallout could be severe."

Sheikh Khalid's expression remained calm, but his eyes narrowed slightly. "And if you do not support Pakistan, what then?" he asked. "What happens when Pakistan turns elsewhere for support? To China, perhaps? Or Russia?"

Dean felt a flicker of unease. The mention of China and Russia struck a nerve. He knew that both countries had been quietly courting Pakistan, eager to expand their influence in the region. The Cold War chessboard was always shifting, and Pakistan's strategic position made it a valuable piece in the game.

"We'll see what we can do," Dean replied cautiously, choosing his words carefully. "But there are no guarantees."

The sheikhs nodded, appearing satisfied for the moment, but they exchanged a quick glance, a silent agreement passing between them. They knew they would need to keep the pressure on, to remind the Americans that the stakes were high—and that they were not the only players at the table.

As the meeting adjourned, Sheikh Khalid rose to his feet, extending his hand to Dean. "Thank you for your time," he said smoothly. "I trust that you will make the right decision."

Dean shook his hand, offering a polite smile. "We will do our best," he replied, though his mind was already racing, calculating the implications of their conversation. He knew this was far from over. The sheikhs would not let the matter rest.

As the Arab delegation left the room, Dean turned to his colleagues, his expression serious. "We need to monitor this situation closely," he said. "If the sheikhs are this concerned, there's more going on than we realize. We can't afford to be blindsided."

The others nodded in agreement; their faces set in grim determination. They knew they were walking a tightrope, and one wrong step could plunge them into a crisis that would have far-reaching consequences.

London, UK – A Safe House

A cold drizzle fell over London, the mist clinging to the narrow streets like a shroud. John Harrison and Peter Grant moved quickly through the dark alleyways; their collars turned up against the chill. They were headed to a safe house—a nondescript flat in a quiet part of the city, far from the prying eyes of their colleagues at MI5 and the CIA.

The flat was sparsely furnished, the walls bare except for a few maps and documents pinned haphazardly around the room. A single lamp cast a pool of light over a small table covered with files, photographs, and a laptop that hummed quietly in the corner.

Grant closed the door behind them, locking it carefully. "We're running out of time," he said, his voice low, almost a whisper. "They're onto us, John. I can feel it."

Harrison nodded; his expression grim. "I know," he replied. "But we're too close to stop now. We've uncovered too much. If we back down, they'll bury this forever."

Grant sighed, running a hand through his hair. "What exactly have we got?" he asked, though he knew the answer. "We have bits and pieces, whispers, and rumors. Enough to get us into trouble but not enough to blow the lid off this whole operation."

Harrison moved to the table, picking up a photograph of a meeting in Islamabad—a grainy black-and-white image of Pakistani officials shaking hands with a figure they hadn't yet identified. "It's more than that," he said. "We have evidence that elements within our own agencies are aiding Pakistan's nuclear efforts. 'The Committee,' as they call themselves, are feeding false intelligence, manipulating us. And they have high-level clearance."

Grant shook his head. "It's madness," he said. "A rogue faction within MI5 and the CIA helping Pakistan to get the bomb to counterbalance

Soviet influence in the region? If we go public with this, it will cause an uproar."

Harrison leaned forward; his eyes intense. "That's exactly what they're counting on—that we'll be too scared to act, too worried about the fallout to expose them. But we have to do it. The world needs to know."

Grant hesitated, glancing at the door. "What if they find out what we're doing?" he asked quietly. "What if they come after us?"

Harrison's face hardened. "They're already after us," he said. "We've been under surveillance for weeks. Our phones are tapped, our movements are tracked. But they haven't made a move yet because they think we're still guessing. They don't know how much we've figured out."

Grant nodded slowly, realizing the gravity of their situation. "So, what's the plan?"

Harrison looked at him, his jaw set. "We dig deeper. We find out who's pulling the strings, and we expose them. But we need to be careful—very careful. One wrong step, and we're dead."

Grant swallowed hard, the weight of their mission settling on his shoulders. "Agreed," he said. "But if we're going to do this, we need help—someone on the inside who can feed us information, who knows the players."

Harrison nodded, considering. "I might know someone," he said. "An old contact, someone I trust. But it's a long shot. I'll make the call."

He reached for his phone, his hand trembling slightly. He knew the risks, knew that every move they made could be their last. But he also knew they had no choice. They were too deep in the web now, and the only way out was through.

As he dialed the number, he glanced at Grant. "Whatever happens," he said quietly, "we don't back down. We see this through to the end."

Grant nodded; his expression resolute. "To the end," he echoed.

The phone rang, and Harrison waited, the tension building in the small room. He knew they were about to cross a line, a point of no return. But he also knew that if they didn't act, the conspiracy would continue unchecked, and the world would never know the truth.

Islamabad, Pakistan – ISI Headquarters

Colonel Farooq Siddiqui sat in his office, the dim light from his desk lamp casting long shadows across the room. He had just received the latest intelligence report from his operatives in London. Harrison and Grant were getting too close, digging into places they shouldn't be.

He sighed, leaning back in his chair, his mind racing with the implications. The web of deception that had been carefully woven over the years was beginning to unravel, and if Harrison and Grant succeeded, everything they had worked for would be exposed.

He picked up his phone and dialed a secure number, his voice calm but firm. "It's time," he said simply.

The voice on the other end replied with a single word. "Understood."

Farooq hung up the phone, staring out the window into the dark night. He knew that the next few days would be critical. One wrong move, and the entire operation could collapse. But he had played this game for too long to falter now.

The web was tightening around Harrison and Grant, and Farooq was ready to pull the strings.

Zurich, Switzerland – The Broker's Suite

The Broker sat in his luxurious suite, the lights of the city twinkling outside the large windows. He had just received a message from Kamran, a coded transmission that confirmed the uranium had been successfully secured.

He smiled to himself, sipping his whiskey. The pieces were falling into place, and soon, the final stage of the plan would begin.

But The Broker knew better than anyone that.

in this game, alliances were temporary, and trust was a rare commodity. He had his own plans, his own agenda, and when the time was right, he would make his move.

For now, though, he would wait. The world was on the brink of something big, and The Broker intended to be at the center of it all.

The game was far from over, and The Broker was ready to play his next hand.

Chapter 12: The Final Push

Near the Pakistan-Afghanistan Border – A Treacherous Path

The cold mountain air cut like a knife as Kamran's team moved silently through the darkness. The path wound its way through jagged cliffs and rocky outcrops, barely wide enough for their convoy of three trucks. The vehicles crawled along at a slow, deliberate pace, headlights dimmed to mere slivers of light, barely enough to see a few feet ahead. The night was moonless, the sky a deep, inky black that seemed to swallow sound.

Kamran sat in the lead truck, his eyes scanning the terrain, his senses on high alert. His fingers drummed anxiously on the dashboard; the weight of the mission heavy on his mind. Every sound, every movement in the shadows felt amplified, charged with potential danger. He knew the risks; this was no ordinary road. They were crossing a high-altitude pass near the Pakistan-Afghanistan border, a treacherous route used by smugglers and warlords, notorious for its unpredictability.

In the back of the truck, crates of uranium, carefully shielded and packaged, shifted slightly with every bump and turn. The cargo was precious, highly dangerous, and would be fatal if it fell into the wrong hands. Kamran felt a tightening in his chest as he glanced at his driver, a young, sharp-eyed Pakistani named Faisal. Faisal had served in the army before being recruited for this mission. His hands were steady on the wheel, but Kamran could see the tension in his jaw.

Behind them, in the second truck, a small team of mercenaries traveled with Hajji Mirza, the Afghan warlord they had hired to guide them through this perilous terrain. Mirza had agreed to help them in exchange for a hefty sum, but Kamran had sensed unease since they started the journey. There had been whispers among Mirza's men, furtive glances, and an air of mistrust that Kamran could not shake off.

He turned his head slightly, catching a glimpse of Mirza in the rearview mirror. The warlord's face was partially obscured by the shadows, but Kamran could see his eyes glinting in the dim light, watching, calculating.

Something's off, Kamran thought. He leaned over to his radio and whispered into it, "Stay alert. Keep an eye on Mirza's men. Something doesn't feel right."

His second-in-command, Arif, responded over the crackling radio, his voice low and tense. "Roger that. We're watching them."

Kamran could feel the adrenaline coursing through his veins, his senses heightened, every nerve on edge. He knew they were approaching the narrowest point of the pass—a stretch of road barely wide enough for a single vehicle, with steep cliffs on either side. It was the perfect spot for an ambush.

The trucks slowed even further, their engines rumbling softly. Kamran's eyes flicked between the road ahead and the shadows that clung to the rocks. He felt a bead of sweat trickle down his temple despite the cold.

"Faisal," he whispered to the driver, "be ready for anything. If I say go, you floor it. No hesitation."

Faisal nodded; his eyes fixed on the road.

As they rounded a sharp bend, the headlights illuminated a narrow, steep pass ahead. The cliffs loomed high on either side, and the wind howled through the rocks, a mournful, eerie sound that set Kamran's teeth on edge.

And then he saw it—a flicker of movement in the darkness above. He reached for his radio, but it was too late.

Near the Pakistan-Afghanistan Border – The Ambush

A deafening explosion shattered the night, the sound echoing off the cliffs like thunder. Kamran's truck lurched violently to the side as the road ahead erupted in a shower of dirt and rock. Faisal slammed on the brakes, the truck skidding to a stop just inches from the edge of the cliff.

"Ambush!" Kamran shouted, grabbing his rifle and leaping out of the truck.

From the shadows above, Mirza's men emerged, weapons drawn, their faces twisted with greed and malice. They had been lying in wait, ready to strike. Kamran's team scrambled out of the vehicles, taking cover behind the trucks, their guns raised.

Hajji Mirza stepped forward, a cruel smile on his face, his AK-47 aimed directly at Kamran. "You think you can use us, Malik?" he sneered, his voice dripping with contempt. "This uranium is mine now. Hand it over, and maybe I'll let you live."

Kamran's heart pounded in his chest, but his mind was clear. He knew he had to act fast. "Mirza," he called out, keeping his voice steady, "we had a deal. You help us get through, and you get paid. Don't make this mistake."

Mirza laughed, a harsh, guttural sound. "Your money means nothing to me, Malik," he spat. "This uranium is worth more than anything you could offer. Drop your weapons, or I'll kill you all."

Kamran's fingers tightened around his rifle. He could see the tension in his team's eyes, the uncertainty, the fear. But he also knew they were trained, ready for a fight. He had no intention of surrendering.

He glanced at Arif, who nodded subtly. Kamran raised his rifle and fired a single shot, the bullet whizzing past Mirza's head, a deliberate miss. "Stand down!" he shouted, his voice commanding. "Or we will fight."

Mirza hesitated for a split second, surprised by Kamran's boldness. But then his face hardened, and he raised his AK-47. "Kill them!" he roared.

The air exploded with gunfire as both sides opened up. Bullets ricocheted off rocks, sparks flying in the darkness. Kamran dropped to the ground, returning fire, his eyes scanning the chaos. He could see Mirza's men moving in from both sides, trying to flank them.

"Faisal!" Kamran shouted. "Get the truck moving! Now!"

Faisal scrambled into the driver's seat, turning the key. The engine roared to life, and he slammed on the gas, the truck lurching forward, tires screeching against the rocky ground.

"Arif, cover him!" Kamran shouted, firing off another burst.

Arif nodded, laying down suppressing fire as the truck barreled forward, smashing through a makeshift barricade. Kamran could see Mirza's men scattering, some diving for cover, others firing wildly.

Kamran felt a sharp pain in his shoulder as a bullet grazed him, but he ignored it, focusing on the fight. He knew they had to keep moving, had to break through the ambush, or they would be overrun.

"Move, move!" he shouted to his team, signaling them to follow the truck.

They fought their way forward, inch by inch, bullets flying, rocks exploding around them. Kamran's mind was a blur of adrenaline and instinct, his training kicking in. He could hear the shouts and curses of Mirza's men, the crack of gunfire, the roar of the truck's engine.

Finally, they reached the end of the pass, the road opening up into a wider valley. Faisal floored the gas, the truck accelerating, and Kamran's team jumped onto the back, scrambling for cover.

Mirza shouted something in Pashto, and his men began to retreat, realizing they had lost the element of surprise. Kamran fired a few more shots, then signaled his team to hold fire.

As they sped away, Kamran knew they had survived, but at a cost. They had lost time, ammunition, and a few of their men were wounded. The mission was still in jeopardy, and they were far from safe.

Islamabad, Pakistan – A Secret Bunker

Kamran returned to Islamabad, his body aching from the ordeal, his anger simmering beneath the surface. He had been betrayed, and he needed answers.

He was escorted to a secret bunker, deep beneath the city, where Colonel Farooq Siddiqui was waiting. The room was cold, the air thick with tension. Farooq sat behind a metal desk; his face impassive.

Kamran slammed his hands on the desk, leaning forward. "You've been playing me," he accused, his voice low but furious. "Using me as a pawn."

Farooq remained calm, his gaze steady. "We all play our parts, Kamran," he replied. "But remember, you chose this path."

Kamran's eyes blazed with anger. "You knew Mirza would turn on us," he said. "You sent us into a trap."

Farooq shrugged slightly. "I suspected he might," he admitted. "But we needed to know who we could trust. And now we do."

Kamran clenched his fists, struggling to control his rage. "You've put us all at risk," he said. "For what? To test my loyalty?"

Farooq leaned back in his chair; his expression unreadable. "This is bigger than you or me, Kamran," he said quietly. "Bigger than any one man. You know that."

Kamran knew Farooq was right, but it didn't make the betrayal sting any less. He took a deep breath, trying to steady himself. "What's the next move?" he asked finally.

Farooq smiled faintly. "We keep going," he replied. "But this time, we play by our own rules."

Kamran nodded slowly, his resolve hardening.

He decided then and there that he would see the mission through to the end, but he would no longer trust anyone—not even Farooq. From now on, he would play his own game, and he would play it to win.

Chapter 13: The Aftermath

Islamabad, Pakistan – A Secret Meeting Room

The room was dim, the only light coming from a single, flickering bulb that hung from the ceiling, casting long shadows against the cracked walls. The air was thick with the smell of damp and dust, mingling with the faint scent of tobacco that clung to the walls like a ghost. The door was closed, its wooden frame warped from years of neglect, and a thin line of light seeped through the gap beneath it, hinting at the world outside.

Kamran Malik sat at a small, battered table in the center of the room. He leaned forward, his elbows resting on the scarred surface, his hands clasped together, his fingers steepled as if in prayer. His face was etched with lines of worry and fatigue, his eyes hollow, dark circles beneath them. He had not slept in days, perhaps weeks, and his mind was a labyrinth of conflicting thoughts and emotions.

He stared at the blank sheet of paper in front of him, the tip of his pen hovering above it. He had decided to write a letter to his wife, Amina—a letter he wasn't sure he would ever send. It was a confession, of sorts, a final testament to the choices he had made and the reasons he had made them. He knew he might never see her again, might never have the chance to explain in person why he had chosen this path, why he had risked everything.

Kamran began to write, his hand trembling slightly as he formed the first words on the page:

My Dearest Amina,

There are so many things I want to say, but I don't know where to begin. I feel as if I have been living two lives—one for the world to see and another in the shadows. I know I have hurt you, and I know that you may never forgive me for what I have done, but I hope that one day you will understand.

When I left you, I thought I was doing it for the right reasons. I thought I was protecting you, our family, our country. But now I am not so sure. I have crossed lines I never thought I would cross, made deals with men I despise, and done things that I am not proud of. But I did it because I believed it was necessary, because I believed it was the only way to keep us safe.

He paused, his pen hovering above the paper as he tried to find the right words. His mind flashed with images—the faces of the people he had betrayed, the men he had lied to, the secrets he had kept. He felt a surge of guilt, a wave of doubt that threatened to overwhelm him, but he pushed it aside. He had no time for doubt now.

I don't know what will happen next. I don't know if I will survive this or if I will ever see you again. But know that I love you, and that every decision I have made, I made with you in my heart.

Yours always,

Kamran.

He set the pen down, his hand shaking slightly, and folded the letter carefully. He slipped it into an envelope and sealed it, pressing his thumb against the flap. He stared at the envelope for a long moment, then slipped it into his jacket pocket. He didn't know if he would ever send it, but it was enough to know that he had written it, that he had said what needed to be said.

Kamran leaned back in his chair, closing his eyes for a moment. He felt the weight of everything bearing down on him—the lies, the betrayals, the impossible choices. He had been at the center of a web of intrigue that spanned continents, and now that web was tightening around him. He had made enemies on all sides—within his own government, among his allies, and even within the shadowy circles that had aided him. He wasn't sure who he could trust anymore, or if he could trust anyone at all.

A knock at the door startled him. He opened his eyes and turned his head, his muscles tensing. The door creaked open, and a figure stepped inside. It was Colonel Farooq Siddiqui, his face unreadable, his eyes sharp and assessing.

Farooq closed the door behind him and crossed the room, pulling out a chair and sitting down across from Kamran. For a long moment, neither man spoke. The silence hung heavy in the air, charged with unspoken tension.

"Kamran," Farooq said finally, his voice low and measured. "We need to talk."

Kamran nodded, his expression guarded. "I know," he replied. "What's next?"

Farooq leaned forward, resting his forearms on the table. "Things are getting complicated," he said. "We've received word that the Americans and the British are closing in. They know more than they should. We have leaks everywhere."

Kamran's eyes narrowed. "And you think it's me?" he asked.

Farooq shook his head. "No," he replied. "I know you've been loyal. But there are others... people we trusted who may not be as committed to our cause."

Kamran exhaled slowly, his mind racing. "What do you want from me?"

Farooq's expression softened, and for the first time, Kamran saw a flicker of something like concern in his eyes. "I'm giving you a way out," Farooq said quietly. "A new identity, a chance to disappear. You don't have to see this through, Kamran. You've done enough."

Kamran stared at him, surprised by the offer. "And why would you do that?" he asked.

Farooq hesitated, then spoke with a rare hint of emotion. "Because you're a patriot, Kamran," he said. "Because I know you did this for the right reasons. And because I don't want to see you die."

Kamran shook his head slowly. "No," he said firmly. "I started this. I'll see it through to the end."

Farooq nodded, a look of resignation crossing his face. "Then be careful, Kamran," he warned. "The game is far from over. And the people we're dealing with... they won't hesitate to take you down if they think you're a liability."

Kamran leaned forward, his gaze intense. "I'm no one's liability," he replied. "And I know exactly what I'm doing."

Farooq sighed, then stood up, offering his hand. "Good luck, Kamran," he said. "You're going to need it."

Kamran took his hand, squeezing it tightly. "You too, Colonel," he replied. "You too."

Farooq left the room, and Kamran was alone again. He sat in silence for a long time, his mind racing. He knew he was in deeper than he had ever been before, and he knew that the stakes were higher than ever. But he also knew that he had no choice but to move forward.

Remote Village – Kamran's Hideout

The hideout was a small, remote village nestled in the foothills of the Hindu Kush, far from prying eyes and ears. It was a place where time seemed to stand still, where the days were long and the nights were cold and quiet. Kamran had chosen it for its isolation, its anonymity. Here, he could watch and wait, biding his time.

He sat in a small room with a single window that looked out over the rugged landscape. A small television sat on a rickety table in the corner, the screen flickering with static as it struggled to pick up a signal. Kamran adjusted the antenna, and the image sharpened, revealing a news anchor speaking in urgent tones.

The anchor's voice was tense, her words clipped. "In breaking news, international tensions continue to rise following Pakistan's recent actions. Diplomatic channels remain open, but there are concerns that the situation could escalate further..."

Kamran watched, his face impassive, his mind calculating. He knew that his actions had set off a chain of events that would shape the future of South Asia—and perhaps the world. He had played his part, made his moves, but now he was at the mercy of forces beyond his control.

He picked up a small notebook from the table, flipping through its pages. It was filled with names, dates, contacts—pieces of a puzzle he had been trying to put together for years. He knew he was close, but he also knew that time was running out.

Kamran set the notebook down and picked up the phone, dialing a secure number. He waited, listening to the dial tone, his heart pounding in his chest.

A voice answered on the other end. "Yes?"

"It's Kamran," he said. "Get me The Broker."

There was a pause, and then the voice replied. "One moment."

Kamran waited, his mind racing. He knew he was about to make a dangerous move, but he also knew he had no other choice. He had come too far to turn back now.

The line clicked, and a familiar voice came on the line. "Kamran," The Broker said, his tone cool and measured. "What do you need?"

Kamran took a deep breath, his resolve firm. "It's time for a new deal," he replied. "And I need you to help me make it."

The Broker chuckled softly. "I thought you might say that," he replied. "Tell me more."

Kamran began to speak, outlining his plan, his voice steady and calm. He knew this was his last chance, his final move in a game that had already cost him so much. But he also knew that he was ready, that he would do whatever it took to see it through.

The conversation continued late into the

night, the shadows growing longer as the hours passed. Kamran knew that he was on the edge of something, something that could change everything. And as he spoke, he felt a strange sense of calm wash over him—a sense that, no matter what happened next, he was prepared.

He had made his choices, and he would live—or die—with them.

Epilogue: The Shadows of War

The world reacted to Pakistan's success with a mix of shock, fear, and condemnation. The Arab sheikhs distanced themselves, fearing reprisals. The CIA and MI5 were caught in a web of their own making, their agents left to clean up the mess.

In Washington, D.C., Lisa Connor sat at her desk, reviewing the latest reports. She knew that the game was far from over.

Zurich, Switzerland – The Broker's Suite

The Broker received a call from Kamran. "I need your help," Kamran said.

The Broker smiled. "I thought you might," he replied. "What's the new deal?"

Kamran watched as the world grappled with the reality of a nuclear-armed Pakistan. He knew he had set something in motion that could not be undone.

But he also knew he was ready for whatever came next.

"Let's get started," he said, picking up the phone once more.

About the Author

Syed Makki Shah is an avid follower of global events. The history of the Pakistani Nukes, is one he has followed from a young age.